JULIUS (ANT) eater, MISUNDERSTOOD

LYNN ROWE REED

A DEBORAH BRODIE BOOK, ROARING BROOK PRESS, BROOKFIELD, CONNECTICUT

Copyright © 2005 by Lynn Rowe Reed
A Deborah Brodie Book
Published by Roaring Brook Press
Roaring Brook Press is a division of Holtzbrinck Publishing Holdings Limited Partnership
2 Old New Milford Road, Brookfield, Connecticut 06804

Distributed in
Canada by H. B. Fenn
and Company Ltd.

Roaring Brook Press books are available for
special promotions and premiums.
For details contact: Director of Special Markets,
Holtzbrinck Publishers.

First edition 2005
Printed in the United States of America
2 4 6 8 10 9 7 5 3 1

Library of Congress Cataloging-in-Publication Data
Reed, Lynn Rowe.
Julius Anteater, misunderstood / Lynn Rowe Reed.—1st ed.
p. cm.
"A Deborah Brodie book."
Summary: All Julius Anteater wants is some ants for lunch, but when people
misunderstand his intentions he winds up frightening a school bus driver,
being thrown out of the zoo, and chased by the police.
ISBN 1-59643-042-7
[1. Anteaters—Fiction. 2. Miscommunication—Fiction. 3. Stories in rhyme.] I. Title.
PZ8.3.R2483Ju 2004 [E]—dc22 2003022470

ROARING BROOK PRESS

FOR:
MY DAD,
CHARLIE
ROWE

I just stopped by for a quick bite.

It's schooltime for us,

so we take the bus.

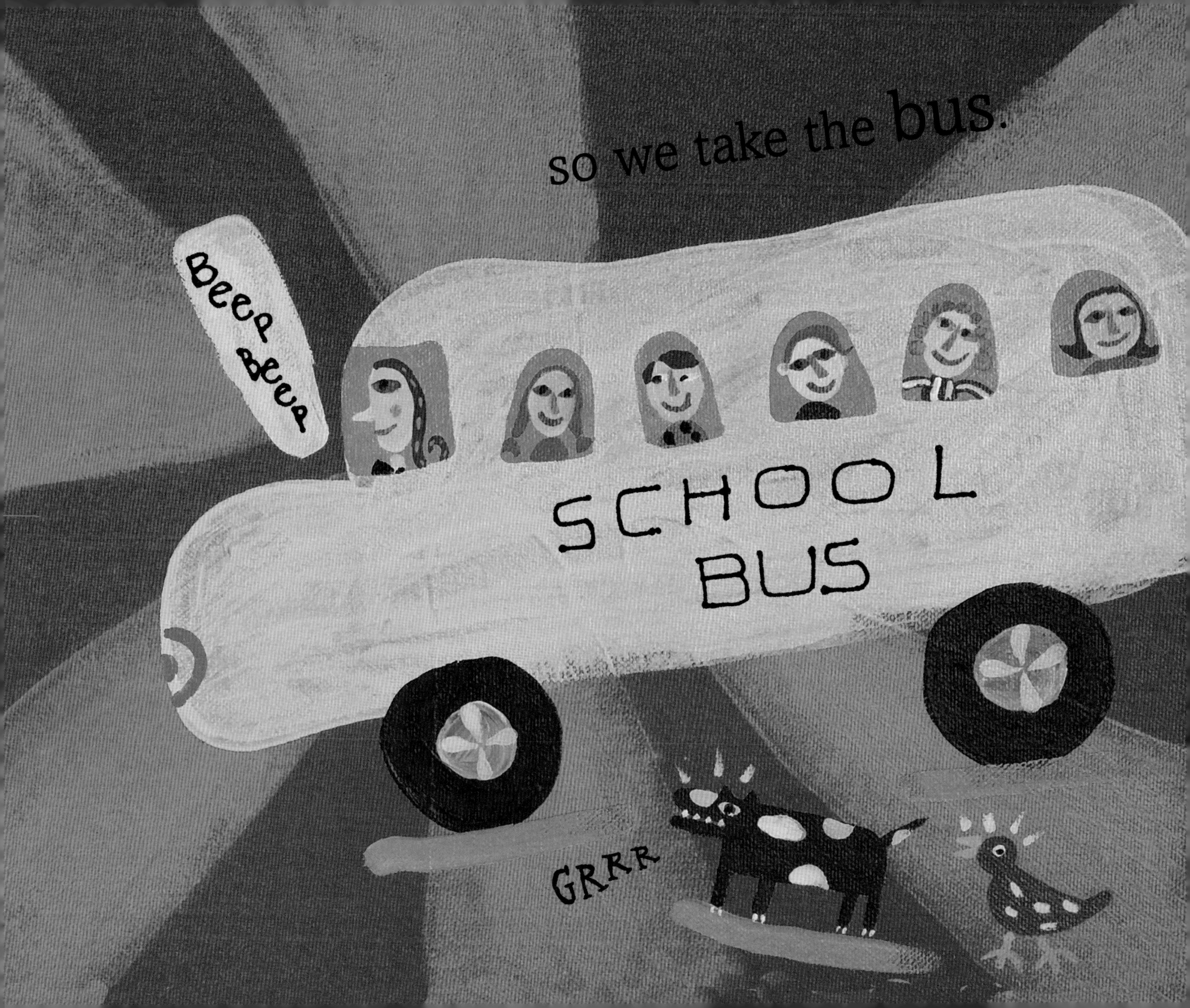

School
ruled!

3 FACTS
ABOUT
ANTEATERS:

(1) The average anteater weighs 100 pounds and is 7 feet from nose to tail!

(2) An anteater eats 30,000 ants, termites and other insects each day

(3) An anteater's tongue is 24 inches LONG.

At two,

We took a field trip to the zoo.

ANTS

→

I had a hunch
I'd get **ants** for lunch.

ELEPHANTS

ELEPHANTS

←

Ants?

Is something here askance?

When I looked
for food,

Suddenly, the car gave chase.

The town came out with its band.

But all I really want
is a truck
full of sand . . .

and an ANT.